CHILDREN'S 21 day loan

PLACE IN RETURN BOX to remove this checkout from your record.
TO AVOID FINES return on or before date due.
MAY BE RECALLED with earlier due date if reqeusted.

DATE DUE	DATE DUE	DATE DUE
CCT 0 9 2014		
1 0 0 1 1 4		
OCT 2 3 2014		
1 1 0 7 1 4		
0 6 1 3 1 5		
1 0 2 3 1 6		

11/13 K:/Proj/Acc&Pres/CIRC/DateDueForms_2013.indd - pg.10

D1446137

THE STEADFAST
TIN SOLDIER

For Aidan, Fionnuala and Aodhán

PZ
8
.A542
St
2005

First published in Great Britain in 1991 by Andersen Press Ltd.,
20 Vauxhall Bridge Road, London SW1V 2SA.
This paperback edition first published in 2005 by Andersen Press Ltd.
Published in Australia by Random House Australia Pty.,
Level 3, 100 Pacific Highway, North Sydney, NSW 2060.
Text copyright © Naomi Lewis, 1986. Illustrations copyright © P.J. Lynch, 1991
The rights of Naomi Lewis and P.J. Lynch to be identified as the author and illustrator of this work have been asserted
by them in accordance with the Copyright, Designs and Patents Act, 1988.
All rights reserved. Colour separated in Switzerland by Photolitho AG, Zürich.
Printed and bound in Italy by Grafiche AZ, Verona.

10   9   8   7   6   5   4

British Library Cataloguing in Publication Data available.

ISBN 978 1 84270 443 1

This book has been printed on acid-free paper.

THE STEADFAST TIN SOLDIER

Hans Christian Andersen

Translated by Naomi Lewis
Illustrated by P.J. Lynch

Andersen Press • London

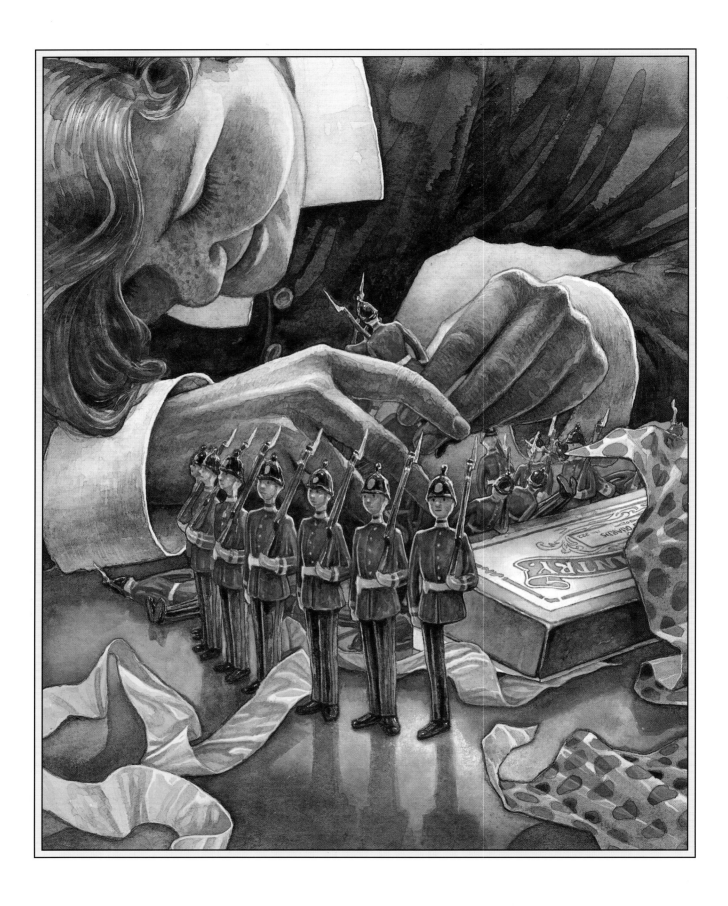

THERE were once twenty-five tin soldiers, all of them brothers, for they had been made from the same tin kitchen spoon. They shouldered arms and looked straight before them, very smart in their red and blue uniforms. "Tin soldiers!" That was the very first thing that they heard in this world, when the lid of their box was taken off. A little boy had shouted this and clapped his hands; he had been given them as a birthday present, and now he set them out on the table. Each soldier was exactly like the next—except for one, which had only a single leg; he was the last to be moulded, and there was not quite enough tin left. Yet he stood just as well on his one leg as the others did on their two, and he is this story's hero.

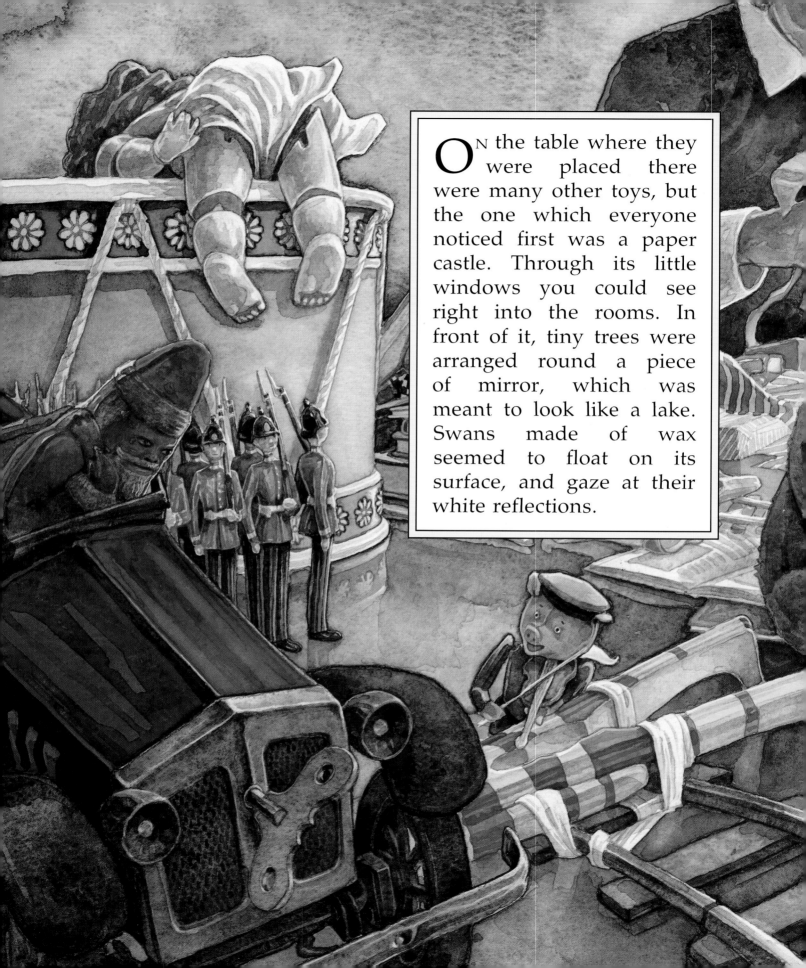

ON the table where they were placed there were many other toys, but the one which everyone noticed first was a paper castle. Through its little windows you could see right into the rooms. In front of it, tiny trees were arranged round a piece of mirror, which was meant to look like a lake. Swans made of wax seemed to float on its surface, and gaze at their white reflections.

THE whole scene was enchanting—and the prettiest thing of all was a girl who stood in the open doorway; she too was cut out of paper, but her gauzy skirt was of finest muslin; a narrow blue ribbon crossed her shoulder like a scarf, and was held by a shining sequin almost the size of her face. This charming little creature held both of her arms stretched out, for she was a dancer; indeed, one of her legs was raised so high in the air that the tin soldier could not see it at all; he thought that she had only one leg like himself.

"Now she would be just the right wife for me," he thought. "But she is so grand; she lives in a castle, and I have only a box—and there are five-and-twenty of us in that! There certainly isn't room for her. Still, I can try to make her acquaintance." So he lay down full length behind a snuff-box which was on the table; from there he could easily watch the little paper dancer, who continued to stand on one leg without losing her balance.

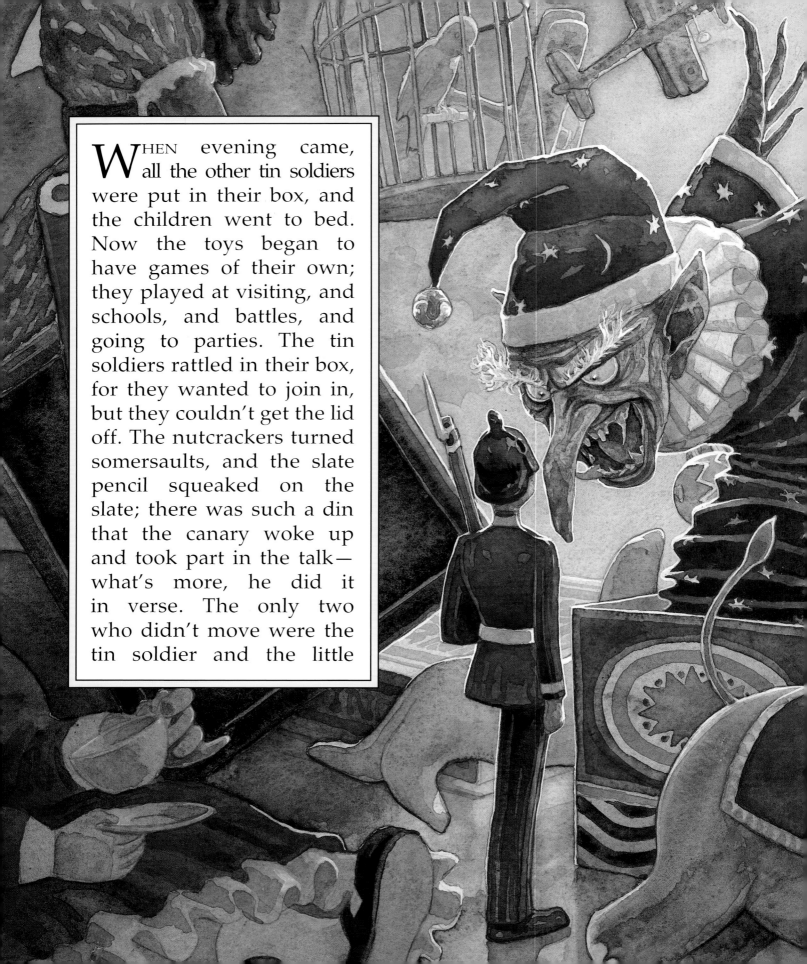

WHEN evening came, all the other tin soldiers were put in their box, and the children went to bed. Now the toys began to have games of their own; they played at visiting, and schools, and battles, and going to parties. The tin soldiers rattled in their box, for they wanted to join in, but they couldn't get the lid off. The nutcrackers turned somersaults, and the slate pencil squeaked on the slate; there was such a din that the canary woke up and took part in the talk—what's more, he did it in verse. The only two who didn't move were the tin soldier and the little

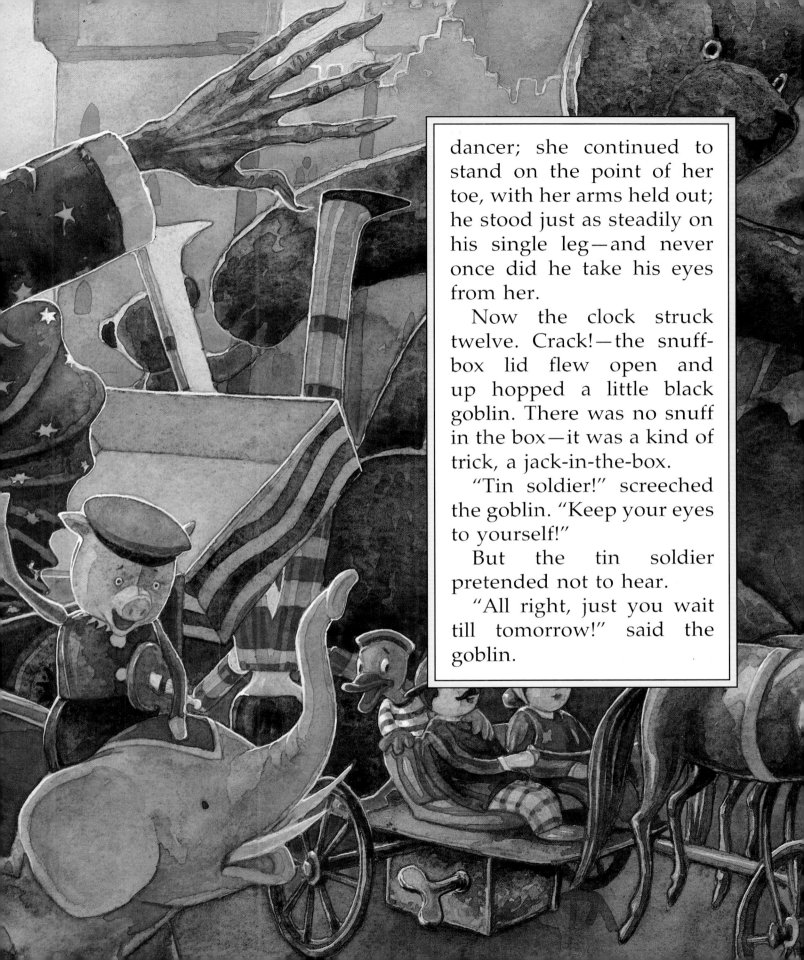

dancer; she continued to stand on the point of her toe, with her arms held out; he stood just as steadily on his single leg—and never once did he take his eyes from her.

Now the clock struck twelve. Crack!—the snuff-box lid flew open and up hopped a little black goblin. There was no snuff in the box—it was a kind of trick, a jack-in-the-box.

"Tin soldier!" screeched the goblin. "Keep your eyes to yourself!"

But the tin soldier pretended not to hear.

"All right, just you wait till tomorrow!" said the goblin.

WHEN morning came and the children were up again, the tin soldier was placed on the window ledge. The goblin may have been responsible, or perhaps a draught blowing through — anyhow, the window suddenly swung open, and out fell the tin soldier, all the three storeys to the ground. It was a frightful fall! His leg pointed upwards, his head was down, and he came to a halt with his bayonet stuck between the paving stones.

THE servant-girl and the little boy went to search in the street, but although they were almost treading on the soldier they somehow failed to see him. If he had called out, "Here I am!" they would have found him easily, but he didn't think it proper behaviour to cry out when he was in uniform.

Now it began to rain; the drops fell fast—it was a drenching shower. When it was over, a pair of urchins passed. "Look!" said one of them. "There's a tin soldier. Let's put him out to sea."

So they made a boat out of newspaper and put the tin soldier in the middle, and set it in the fast-flowing gutter at the edge of the street. Away he sped, and the two boys ran beside him clapping their hands. Goodness, what waves there were in that gutter-stream, what rolling tides! It had been a real downpour. The paper boat tossed up and down, sometimes whirling round and round, until the soldier felt quite giddy. But he remained as steadfast as ever, not moving a muscle, still looking straight in front of him, still shouldering arms.

All at once the boat entered a tunnel under the pavement. Oh, it was dark, quite as dark as it was in the box at home. "Wherever am I going now?" the tin soldier wondered. "Yes, it must be the goblin's doing. Ah! If only that young lady were here with me in the boat, I wouldn't care if it were twice as dark."

SUDDENLY, from its home in the tunnel, out rushed a large water-rat. "Have you a passport?" it demanded. "No entry without a passport!"

But the tin soldier never said a word; he only gripped his musket more tightly than ever. The boat rushed onwards, and behind it rushed the rat in fast pursuit. Ugh! How it ground its teeth, and yelled to the sticks and straws, "Stop him! Stop him! He hasn't paid his toll! He hasn't shown his passport!"

THERE was no stopping the boat, though, for the stream ran stronger and stronger. The tin soldier could just see a bright glimpse of daylight far ahead where the end of the tunnel must be, but at the same time he heard a roaring noise which well might have frightened a bolder man. Just imagine! At the end of the tunnel the stream thundered down into a great canal. It was as dreadful for him as a plunge down a giant waterfall would be for us.

But how could he stop? Already he was close to the terrible edge. The boat raced on, and the poor tin soldier held himself as stiffly as he could—no one could say of him that he even blinked an eye. Suddenly the little vessel whirled round three or four times, and filled with water right to the brim; what could it do but sink! The tin soldier stood in water up to his neck.

DEEPER and deeper sank the boat, softer and softer grew the paper, until at last the water closed over the soldier's head. He thought of the lovely little dancer whom he would never see again, and in his ears rang the words of a song:

Onward, onward, warrior brave!
Fear not danger, nor the grave.

Then the paper boat collapsed entirely. Out fell the tin soldier—and he was promptly swallowed up by a fish.

OH, how dark it was in the fish's stomach! It was even worse than the tunnel, and very much more cramped. But the tin soldier's courage remained unchanged; there he lay, as steadfast as ever, his musket still at his shoulder. The fish swam wildly about, twisted and turned, and then became quite still. Something flashed through like a streak of lightning—then all around was cheerful daylight, and a voice cried out, "The tin soldier!" The fish had been caught, taken to market, sold and carried into the kitchen, where the cook had cut it open with a large knife. Now she picked up the soldier, holding him round his waist between her finger and thumb, and took him into the living room, so that all the family could see the remarkable character who had travelled about inside a fish.

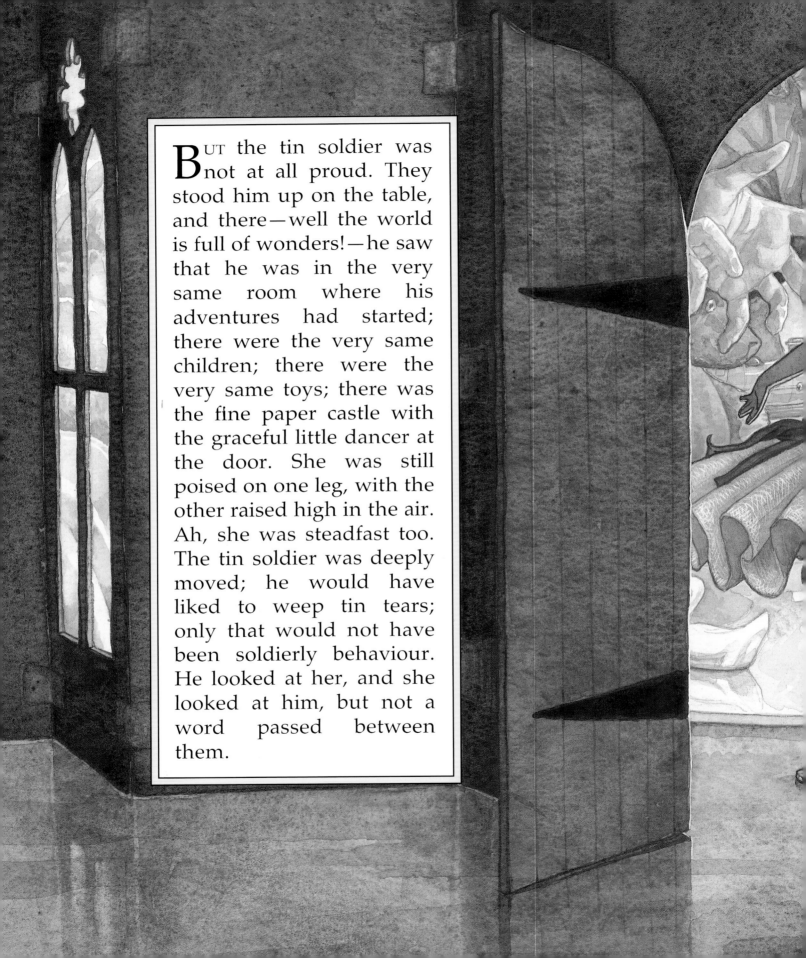

But the tin soldier was not at all proud. They stood him up on the table, and there—well the world is full of wonders!—he saw that he was in the very same room where his adventures had started; there were the very same children; there were the very same toys; there was the fine paper castle with the graceful little dancer at the door. She was still poised on one leg, with the other raised high in the air. Ah, she was steadfast too. The tin soldier was deeply moved; he would have liked to weep tin tears; only that would not have been soldierly behaviour. He looked at her, and she looked at him, but not a word passed between them.

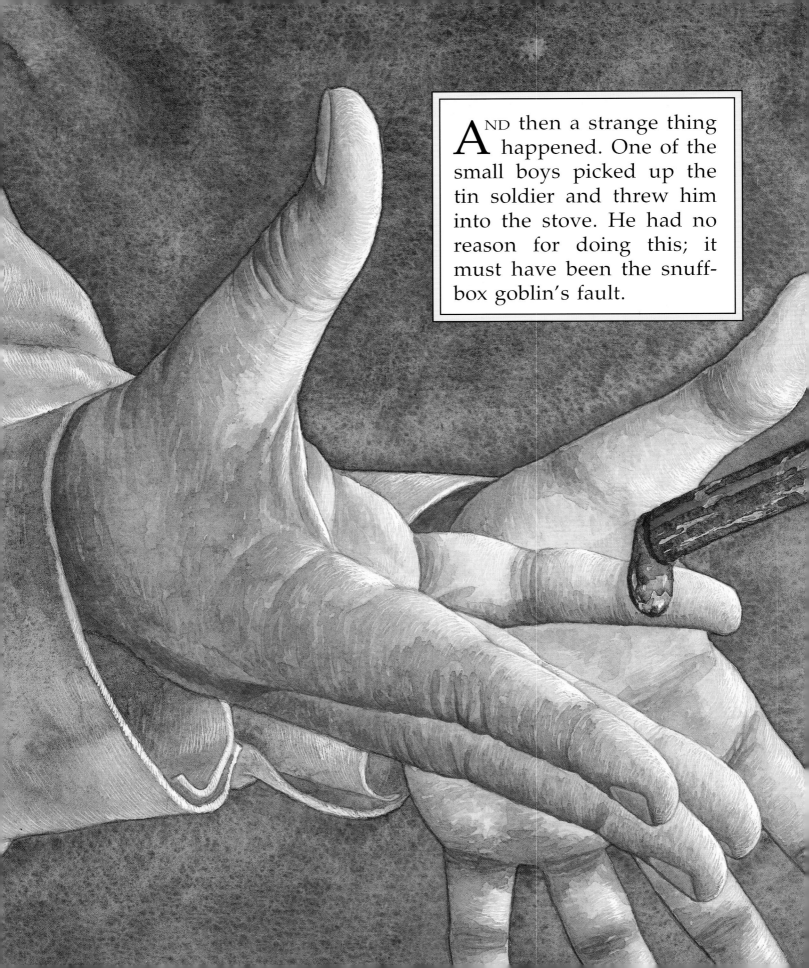

AND then a strange thing happened. One of the small boys picked up the tin soldier and threw him into the stove. He had no reason for doing this; it must have been the snuff-box goblin's fault.

THE tin soldier stood framed in a blaze of light. The heat was intense, but whether this came from the fire or his burning love, he could not tell. His bright colours were now gone—but whether they had been washed away by his journey, or through his grief, none could say. He looked at the pretty little dancer, and she looked at him; he felt that he was melting away, but he still stood steadfast, shouldering arms. Suddenly the door flew open; a gust of air caught the little paper girl, and she flew like a sylph right into the stove, straight to the waiting tin soldier; there she flashed into flame and vanished.

THE soldier presently melted down to a lump of tin, and the next day, when the maid raked out the ashes, she found him—in the shape of a little tin heart. And the dancer? All they found was her sequin, and that was as black as soot.